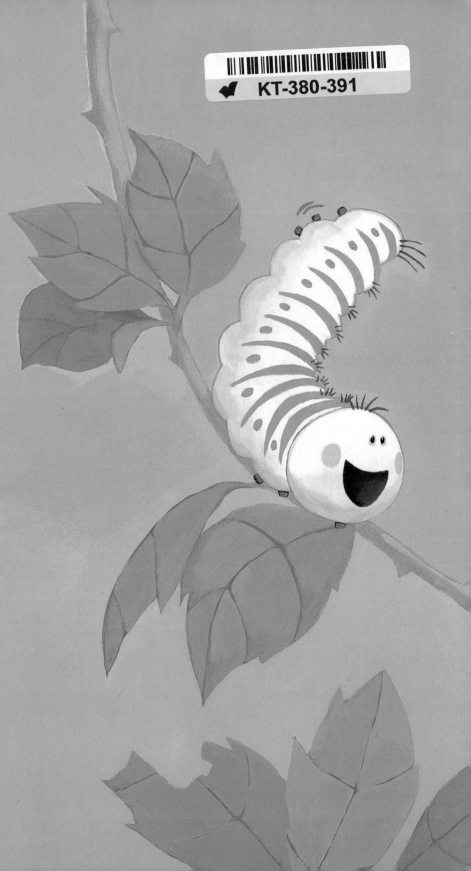

This Little Tiger book belongs to:

_____

_____

_____

_____

LITTLE TIGER PRESS
1 The Coda Centre, 189 Munster Road,
London SW6 6AW
www.littletiger.co.uk
First published in Great Britain 2000
This edition published 2016
Text copyright © Sheridan Cain 2000
Illustrations copyright © Jack Tickle 2000
Visit Jack Tickle at www.ChapmanandWarnes.com
Sheridan Cain and Jack Tickle have asserted their rights
to be identified as the author and illustrator of this work
under the Copyright, Designs and Patents Act, 1988.
All rights reserved
ISBN 978-1-84869-380-7
Printed in China • LTP/1900/1740/1216
10 9 8 7 6 5 4 3 2

For my family
~SC
For Jim and Raechele
~JT

The Crunching Munching Caterpillar

Sheridan Cain

Jack Tickle

LITTLE TIGER PRESS
London

Caterpillar was always hungry.
For weeks he crunched and munched
his way through the fresh,
juicy leaves of a blackberry bush.

Bzzzzzzzz

One day, Caterpillar was about to
crunch into another leaf when . . .

Bzzzzzzzzzzzzz

Bumblebee landed
beside him!

"Wow!" said Caterpillar,
"how did you get here?"
"Simple," said Bumblebee,
"I have wings. Look!"
"Oh, I'd like some of those,"
said Caterpillar.

Bumblebee flew up into the air and buzzed busily from flower to flower.

Bzzzzz

Bzzzz

"I'd love to fly like that,"
said Caterpillar.
"Well, you can't," said Bumblebee.
"I've got wings, and you've got legs.
Your legs are for walking."
"I guess so," sighed Caterpillar.

Bzzzzzoommm

Bumblebee flew off to the next bush.
Watching Bumblebee fly had made
Caterpillar *very* hungry, so he
crunched and he munched
until it was time for bed.

crunch Munch
crunch Munch
yaw-w-n!

Caterpillar woke to
the sound of twittering.
Birds swooped and soared
in the early morning light.

Caterpillar was just about to start
his breakfast when . . .

. . . Sparrow landed
beside him.

"I'd love to fly high in the air like that," said Caterpillar.

"Well, you can't," said Sparrow. "You need to be as light as the dandelion clock that floats on the breeze. You're far too fat to fly. Your legs are for walking."

"I guess so," said Caterpillar glumly.

Caterpillar carried on crunch-munching
all day, until the light began to dim.

crunch
Munch

crunch
Munch

He wrapped a leaf around himself to keep warm.
He was just about to go to sleep when . . .

Butterfly landed gracefully beside him.

"Oh, I wish I could fly like you," sighed Caterpillar.
"But I'm too fat and I have legs instead of wings."
Butterfly smiled a secret, knowing smile.
"Who knows? Perhaps one day you will fly,
light as a feather, like me," she said.
"But now, little Caterpillar, you should
go to sleep. You look very tired."

Butterfly was right. Caterpillar
suddenly felt very sleepy.
As Butterfly flew off into the
night sky, he fell into a deep,
deep sleep.

Caterpillar slept all through the winter,
and his sleep was filled with dreams.

He dreamed he had wings and was soaring in the blue sky above the tall trees . . . .

He dreamed he was a dandelion clock, drifting towards the sun.

He dreamed he was as light as a feather, floating on the breeze.

When Caterpillar woke up he felt
the warmth of the spring sun.
He was stiff from his long sleep,
but he did not feel very hungry.

He stretched and stretched...

... and a breeze lifted
Caterpillar into the air.

He was no longer
short and plump.
He had WINGS!
Great, big, wonderful
BUTTERFLY WINGS!

"Wow!" said Young Butterfly. "I'm flying! I'm really flying!"

CD track 1 – complete story with original music and sound effects
CD track 2 – story with page turn pings encourages learner readers to join in

Running time – over 15 mins • Produced by The Complete Works, Warwickshire CV31 1JP,
in conjunction with Stationhouse • Music composed by Jim Betteridge and Sam Park

Visit our website www.littletiger.co.uk for details of other Little Tiger Picture Book
and CD Sets, plus our full catalogue of novelty, board and picture books.